An orbit is the path of one object moving around another object.

A moon orbits a planet.

Planets orbit stars called suns.

Stars come in different sizes.

The smallest stars are called red dwarfs.

The biggest stars are called hypergiants.

Earth is in the solar system which is in the Milky Way galaxy.

Comets are chunks of rock, ice, dust, and gas zooming through outer space.

There are over 200 billion stars in the Milky Way galaxy.

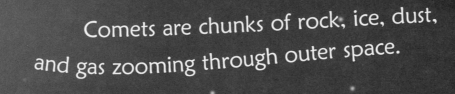
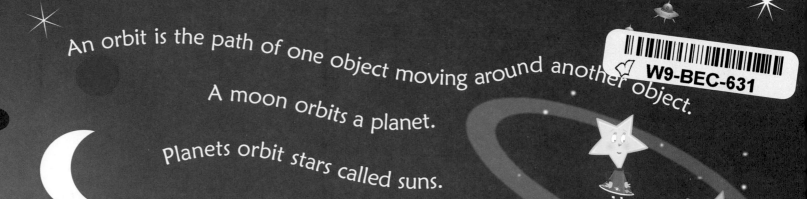

TWINKLE, STAR OF THE WEEK

Joan Holub

Illustrated by

Paul Nicholls

Albert Whitman & Company, Chicago, Illinois

Library of Congress Cataloging-in-Publication Data

Holub, Joan.
Twinkle, star of the week / by Joan Holub ; illustrated by Paul Nicholls.
p. cm.
Summary: Twinkle, the sparkliest student in Sky School, looks forward to her turn to be "Star of the Week,"
but when another student sings the song Twinkle has been practicing, she must find something else to share.
ISBN 978-0-8075-8131-5
[1. Stars—Fiction. 2. Schools—Fiction. 3. Wishes—Fiction.] I. Nicholls, Paul, ill. II. Title.
PZ7.H7427Twi 2010 [E]—dc22 2009024939

10 9 8 7 6 5 4 3 2 1 BP 14 13 12 11 10 09

The design is by Carol Gildar.
Mr. Nicholls first did pencil sketches, then completed the art digitally.

For more information about Albert Whitman & Company, please visit our web site at www.albertwhitman.com.

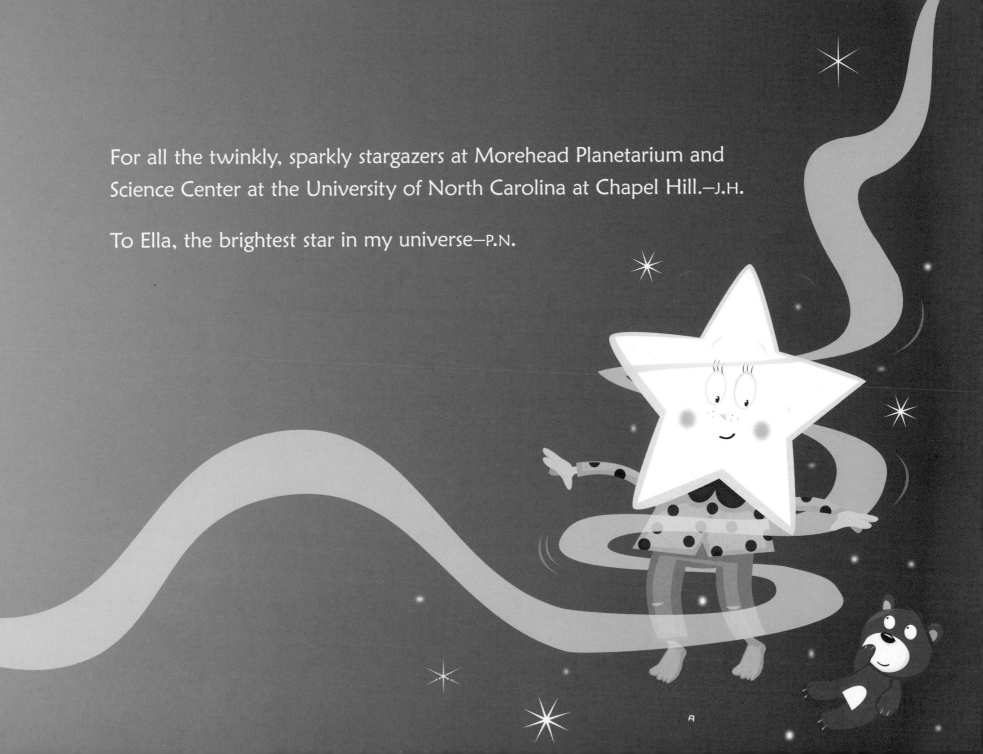

For all the twinkly, sparkly stargazers at Morehead Planetarium and Science Center at the University of North Carolina at Chapel Hill.—J.H.

To Ella, the brightest star in my universe—P.N.

Shimmer

Dazzle

One day in Sky School, Ms. Sun told her class, "You will each get a turn to be Star of the Week. During your week, you will be my helper. You'll get to sit in the Milky Way chair, and you'll be the superstar of Sharing Time."

MILKY WAY

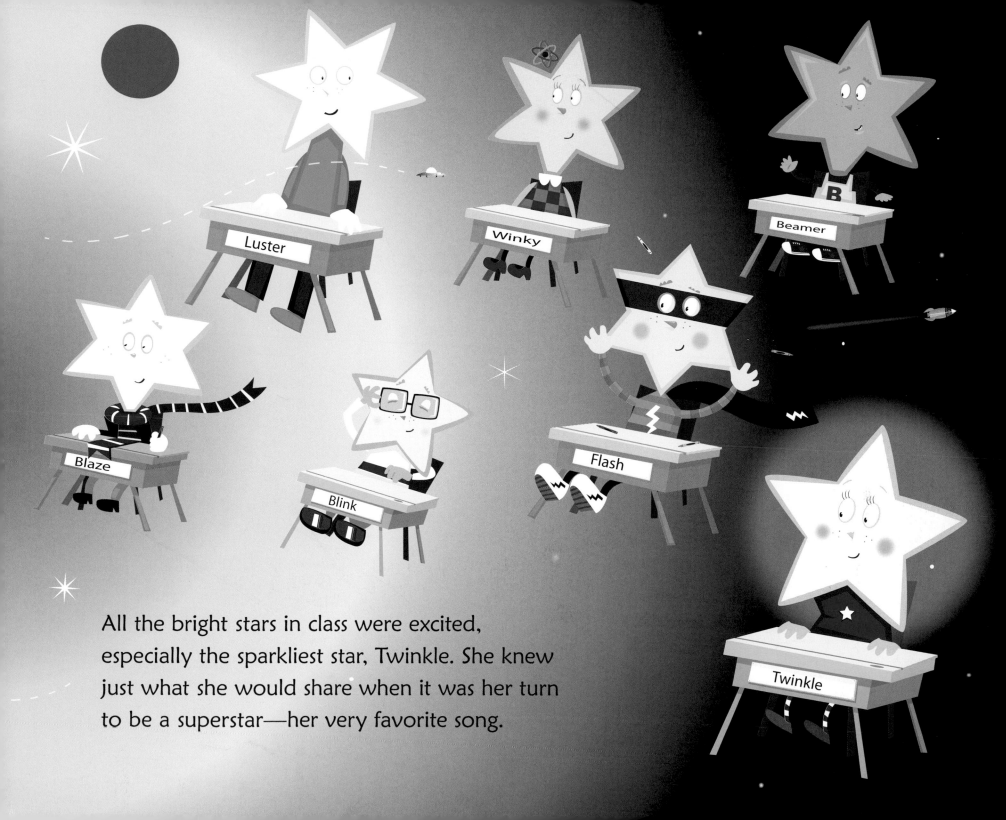

Luster

Winky

Beamer

Blaze

Blink

Flash

Twinkle

All the bright stars in class were excited, especially the sparkliest star, Twinkle. She knew just what she would share when it was her turn to be a superstar—her very favorite song.

But first, it was Dazzle's turn to be Star of the Week. During Sharing Time, she twirled for them. "My planets circle me like a whirling tutu," she said. The class counted three planets around Dazzle.

Around Ms. Sun, they counted eight planets!

At recess, Twinkle practiced the song she would sing when it was her turn. She made three mistakes. *I need more practice*, she thought.

The next week, Blaze got to be the superstar.
He brought asteroid cookies for snack time. Asteroids are mostly rock. Twinkle was glad his cookies were not.

Twinkle

Next Beamer was Star of the Week.

He brought a mystery sack to class. It wiggled and jiggled.

"Guess what's in my sack," he said.

"Does it have a planet tutu?" asked Dazzle.

"No, but it does have a tail," said Beamer.

Suddenly, the bag gave an extra-hard wiggle.

It burst open! Something streaked across the sky. "It's my pet, Comet!" Beamer shouted. Everyone cheered as he chased after it.

That night, Twinkle practiced her song again.
This time, she only made two mistakes.
My song is getting better, she thought.
But it's not ready to share yet.

Soon it was Shimmer's turn to be Star of the Week.
She got to lead the line to recess.

She shared her favorite game,
where the stars made shapes.
It was called Constellation Tag.

As the weeks passed, the other stars had their turns.

Winky helped Ms. Sun decorate the bulletin board.

Luster read his favorite book.

Flash showed his collection.

Twinkle kept practicing.
Soon she didn't make
a single mistake.
Her song was perfect.
In only one more week,
she would sing it for the class!

But before Twinkle, it was Blink's turn to sit in the Milky Way chair. When everyone gathered around, he said, "I have a favorite song."

He began to sing:

"Twinkle, twinkle, little star,
how I wonder what you are.
Up above the world so high,
like a diamond in the sky.
Twinkle, twinkle, little star,
how I wonder what you are!"

Oh, no! Blink had sung her song!
Twinkle jumped up.
"That's *my* song,"
she said angrily.
"My mom sings it to me."

"But everyone knows 'Twinkle, Twinkle, Little Star,'" said Blink.
The other stars nodded.
"Oh. I thought my mom made it up," Twinkle said in a small voice.

For the rest of the week, Twinkle tried to think of something else to share when her turn came. She couldn't tell about planet tutus. Or bring asteroid cookies or a comet. She couldn't sing the Twinkle song, either. That would look like copying.

Finally it was the night before her turn. What was she going to do?
"I wish I had a new idea," she said to herself over and over.

Suddenly Twinkle heard a small, faraway voice whispering:

"Star light, star bright,
first star I see tonight.
I wish I may, I wish I might
have the wish I wish tonight.

I wish I had a friend."

Someone had sent her a wish!
She felt it whoosh
around her, soft and
hopeful, like a hug.

Twinkle answered, trying her
very best to make it come true:

"Dear Wish Maker, Wish Maker, far away.
To make a friend, ask someone to play."

DEAR WISH MAKER

DEAR WISH MAKER

DEAR W

The minute the words left her,
something wonderful happened.
Her own wish came true.
She got a new idea to share
at school!

The next day, Twinkle sparkled with excitement as she shared her big news. "Last night, I was chosen as a Wishing Star!"

Everyone gasped. All stars hope to be chosen as Wishing Stars.

"How did it happen?" asked Blink.

"Someone sent me a wish," Twinkle explained.

"What was it?" asked Dazzle.

"I can't tell you," said Twinkle,

"because wishes are secrets between

Wish Makers and Wishing Stars."

After that, the other stars lined up
to tell Twinkle their secret wishes.

A Wishing Star must be good at listening and helping, thought Twinkle.
She promised to do her best to make all their wishes come true.

And tonight, if you make a wish on Twinkle, the sparkliest star in the sky, she'll do the same for you!

The sun is the closest star to Earth.

A constellation is a named pattern of stars.

The Big Dipper is part of the constellation Ursa Major.

There are 88 constellations.

Stars are balls of hot gas held together by gravity.

A shooting star is a nickname for a meteor.

Meteors are rock or metal bits streaking into Earth's atmosphere from outer space.

There are 8 planets in our solar system.

The atmosphere and outer space we see from Earth is called sky.